W9-BLP-714

THE TINDERBOX

HANS CHRISTIAN ANDERSEN
ILLUSTRATED BY
WARWICK HUTTON

Margaret K. McElderry Books
NEW YORK

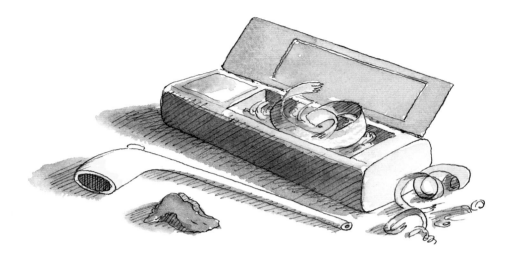

Margaret K. McElderry Books
Macmillan Publishing Company
866 Third Avenue
New York, NY 10022
Collier Macmillan Canada, Inc.

First Edition
Printed in Japan

10 9 8 7 6 5 4 3 2 1

Library of Congress Cataloging-in-Publication Data
Andersen, H. C. (Hans Christian), 1805–1875.
[Fyrtøjet. English]
The tinderbox / Hans Christian Andersen; illustrated by Warwick
Hutton.—1st ed.
p.   cm.
Translation of: Fyrtøjet.
Summary: With the help of a magic tinderbox, a soldier finds a
fortune and pursues a princess imprisoned in a castle.
ISBN 0-689-50458-6
[1. Fairy tales.]   I. Hutton, Warwick, ill.   II. Title.
III. Title: Tinderbox.
PZ8.A542Ti 1988
[E]—dc19   88-9206
CIP   AC

Once upon a time, a soldier came marching along on the highway, with his knapsack on his back and his sword at his side. He was on his way home from the wars.

Presently, in front of him, stood an old witch. She was terribly ugly, and her lower lip hung down over her chin. "Good evening, soldier," she said. "You look fine and strong with your sword and knapsack. How would you like to make a fortune? You see that great tree there?" and she pointed to a stout oak. "Well, its trunk is hollow. If you climb up, you will see a hole, which you can slide down through to the bottom. I'll tie a rope round your waist so I can haul you up when you're ready."

"What do I have to do down in the tree?" asked the soldier.

"Just collect all the money you want," said the witch.
"When you reach the bottom, you'll find yourself in a great
hall, lit by a hundred lamps. There are three doors. When you
go into the first room, there will be a chest with a dog sitting
on it. He has eyes as big as teacups, but don't worry about
that. Just spread my apron on the floor—I'll lend it to you—
and lift him carefully onto it. Then take as many as you want
of the copper coins from the chest. If you'd rather have silver,
go to the next room. There you'll find, sitting on a chest, a
dog with eyes as big as mill wheels. Lift him off in the same
way onto the apron and you can fill your pockets with silver.
The third room has a chest full of gold coins and the dog
there, well, you've never seen such huge eyes. Each is as big
as the Round Tower, but again, just set him on the apron and
you can take what you want."

"But what do *you* want from all this?" asked the soldier.
"I'm sure you're not letting me have all the money for
nothing!"

"Don't worry," said the witch. "I won't take a penny. All I
want is the tinderbox my grandmother left down there."

"All right," said the soldier. And he took the apron, tied the
rope round his waist, and climbed down the tree.

Soon he was standing in the great hall, lit by a hundred lamps, just as the witch had said. When he opened the first door, there was the dog with eyes as big as teacups. "There, there, good dog!" said the soldier, and he lifted it carefully onto the apron. He filled his pockets with copper coins, put the dog back on the chest, and went into the second room.

There sat the dog with eyes as big as mill wheels. "Don't stare at me like that," he said, putting it down on the apron. "It will weaken your eyes." When he saw the heaps of silver in the chest, he threw away the copper coins and filled his pockets and knapsack.

Then he went into the third room. The dog really had eyes as large as the Round Tower, and they rolled around in its head like wheels. "Good evening," said the soldier as he watched the dog in amazement, but he didn't look for long. He lifted the enormous dog onto the apron and opened the chest. At the first sight of such rich treasure, he threw away all the silver and stuffed his pockets and knapsack, cap and boots with gold. He could hardly walk because of the weight, but he set the enormous dog on the chest again, made his way back, and called up the tree, "Pull me up again, old woman!"

"Have you got the tinderbox?" asked the witch.

"I nearly forgot all about it!" the soldier said. So he fetched the box and the witch hauled him up.

"What do you want with that tinderbox?" he asked, when he was up in the open air again.

"Mind your own business. You've got your money, now give me the tinderbox."

"No, I won't," he replied. "If you don't tell me what it's for, I'll cut your head off with my sword!"

"No!" cried the witch. So the soldier cut her head off, and he left her there and strode off. He marched to the nearest town, with the tinderbox in his pocket and all the money tied up in the apron.

It was a large and splendid town. The soldier went to the best lodgings and ordered the best room and the best food. The next day he bought elegant new clothes and was very soon talking and drinking with everyone as if he'd been a wealthy townsman for years. As he talked and listened, he learned about the king, who lived in the town, and his beautiful daughter. It had been foretold that the princess would marry a common soldier, which the king wouldn't hear of, so he kept her safe in a castle surrounded by high walls to guard her from her fate.

"Oh, I'd give the world to see the princess," thought the soldier.

Meanwhile, he lived a merry life. But remembering his own bad times, he was always generous to those less fortunate than himself. As he spent his money so freely, everyone said what a good fellow he was, what a real gentleman.

However, as the weeks passed into months, his money began to run out. He had to leave his lodgings and move into an attic room. He had to clean his own shoes and darn and mend his own clothes. None of his friends visited him anymore,

for they would not climb so many stairs just to see him.

One evening, as it grew dark, he found he had even run out of candles. Remembering that there was an old candle stub in the tinderbox he'd found in the tree, he opened it carefully and struck a light.

As the sparks flew from the flint, the door of his room was thrown open, and there stood the dog with eyes as big as teacups. "What is your command?" it said.

"Well done!" cried the soldier. "What a splendid tinderbox, if I can get what I want with so little trouble. Get me some money!" he told the dog, and almost before he could blink the dog was back with a huge bag of copper pennies in its mouth. Soon the soldier understood how to use the tinderbox. One strike brought the dog that guarded the copper money. Two strikes would bring the dog from the chest full of silver, and three strikes the dog from the chest of gold. The soldier was soon back in the best lodgings, wearing elegant new clothes, and entertaining his friends as before.

"It is very strange," thought the soldier, "that no one may see the beautiful princess." He longed for a glimpse of her, and one night he decided to try the tinderbox. He struck the flint once and when the dog appeared, he said, "I know it's the middle of the night, but I long to see the king's daughter, even if it's only for a minute." The dog rushed off and in a few minutes returned with the princess, who lay stretched out fast asleep on its back. She was exquisitely beautiful. The soldier gazed at her in wonder, then bent forward and kissed her gently. At once, the dog ran back with the princess to her castle.

The next morning at breakfast the princess told the king
and queen of the curious dream she'd had that night: that
she had been carried on the back of a great dog, and that a
man who looked like a soldier had kissed her. "I don't like the
sound of all this," said the queen, and she asked an old lady
of the court to keep watch by the princess's bedside the next
night.

That night the soldier longed to see the beautiful princess
again. The dog was sent and took her on its back once more.
But the clever old woman ran after them. When she saw the
house they entered, she scratched a cross on the front door
with chalk to remember it by. Luckily the dog was just as
clever and on the return journey it noticed the cross. It made
crosses on all the other front doors in town, so no one would
be able to find the right house.

The old lady told her story to the queen and in the
morning the whole court started out to find the house.
"There it is!" said the king. "Don't be silly, it's over here!" said
the queen. But as everyone noticed crosses, they soon gave
up, realizing they'd been tricked.

However, the queen was a clever woman. That day she made a silk bag. She filled it with flour and tied it round the princess's neck. Just before she went to bed, she snipped a small hole in it.

Again that night the dog came for the princess, and as it ran through the town a trail of flour marked its way. The dog did not notice it, so the next morning the soldier was arrested and thrown into jail.

There he sat in darkness. The jailer said, "You'll be hanged from the gallows in the morning." The poor soldier felt all was over and, what was worse, he'd left the tinderbox in his room.

Early the next morning he climbed up to the small prison window. Through the bars he could see the feet of people hurrying off to the execution place to watch the hanging. There were drums and marching soldiers. Among the crowd was a shoemaker's apprentice. He slipped and his shoe flew off just as he was running past the prison window.

"Hey there!" called the soldier. "What are you hurrying
for? The show won't start till I get there! If you will run to my
lodging and get the little tinderbox I left there, I'll give you a
silver coin." And that's just what the boy did.

On the edge of town, a high gallows was set up,
surrounded by soldiers. Hundreds of people filled the field.
The king and queen sat on splendid thrones.

The soldier climbed up and the rope was put round his neck.

As the hangman got ready, the soldier said, "Every condemned man is allowed one small wish before he dies. I should like to smoke a pipe of tobacco before you pull the noose." The king couldn't refuse, so the soldier took out the tinderbox and struck once—struck twice—and struck thrice. Three huge dogs stood before him, one with eyes like teacups, one like mill wheels, and one with eyes like the Round Tower. "Save me, dogs!" cried the soldier to the dogs.

At once they rushed at the judge, the councillors, and the king and queen. They tossed them up in the air and as they tumbled down, they were dashed to pieces. The soldiers were terrified and all the people shouted, "You shall be our king and marry the beautiful princess!"

The soldier climbed down from the scaffold and into the royal carriage, with the three dogs guarding him. The princess was released from her castle and made queen, which she enjoyed very much. The wedding feast lasted for eight days with the three dogs as guests of honor.